Puss in Boots

First published in the United States in 2010
by Picture Window Books
151 Good Counsel Drive
P.O. Box 669
Mankato, Minnesota 56002
www.picturewindowbooks.com

Printed in the United States of America.

All books published by Picture Window Books
are manufactured with paper containing
at least 10 percent post-consumer waste.

Library of Congress Cataloging-in-Publication Data
Piumini, Roberto.
[Gatto con gli stivali. English]
Puss in boots / by Roberto Piumini; illustrated by Francesca Chessa.
p. cm. — (Storybook classics)
ISBN 978-1-4048-5645-5 (library binding)
[1. Fairy tales. 2. Folklore—France.] I. Chessa, Francesca, ill. II. Puss in boots. English. III.
Title.
PZ8.P717Pu 2010
398.20944'04529752—dc22
[E] 2009010463

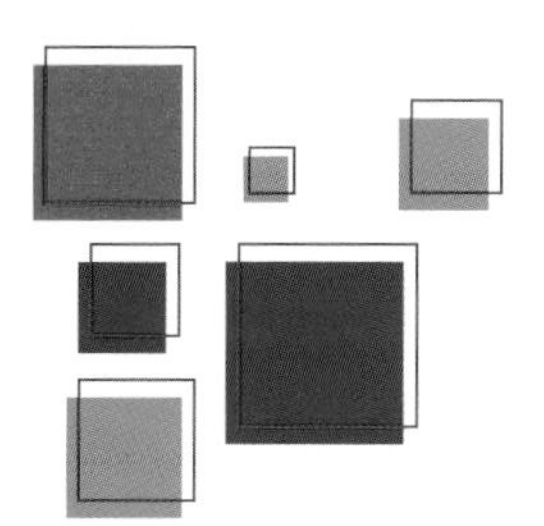

Puss in Boots

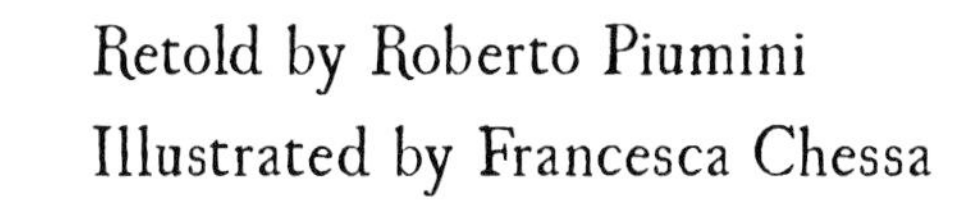
Retold by Roberto Piumini
Illustrated by Francesca Chessa

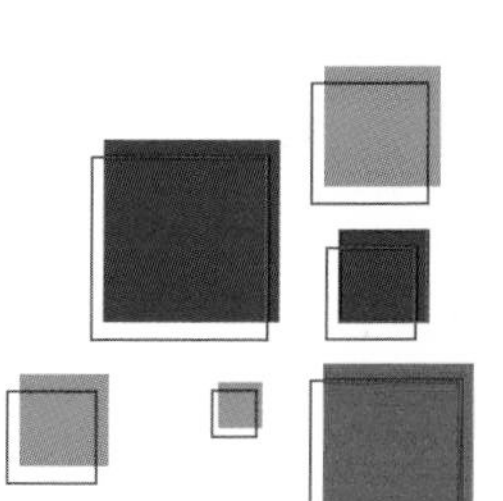

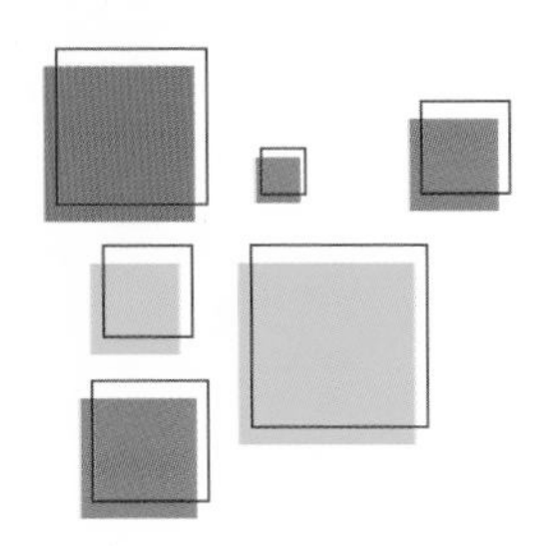

Once upon a time, an old miller rested on his deathbed. He asked to speak with his three sons one last time.

"To my eldest son, I'm leaving the mill," he said. "To my second son, I'm leaving my donkey. And to my third son, I'm leaving the cat."

The third son was disappointed. He looked at the cat and said, "With the mill and the donkey, my brothers will be able to support themselves. But what good is this cat? I will have nothing to eat. Would you even make a decent meal?"

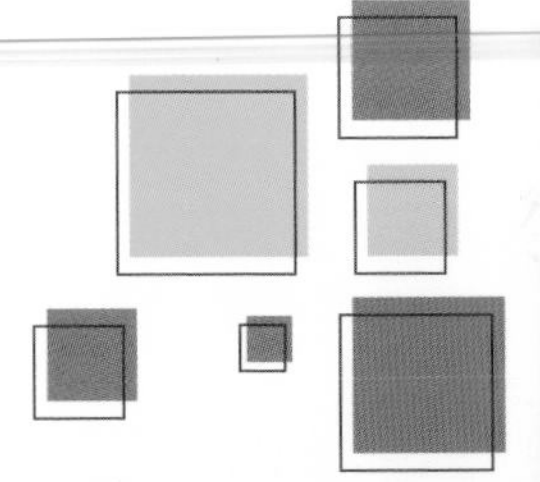

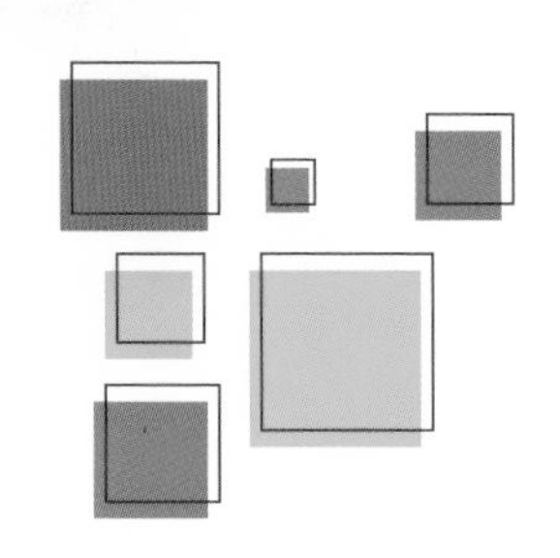

The cat, nervous that he'd be eaten, said, "Master, do not worry. I can help you."

"How?" asked the confused young man.

"Trust me," said the cat. "I will need a nice pair of boots for walking and a cloth bag with no holes in the bottom."

The young man saw how clever the cat was. So he had some boots made for the cat and bought him a bag at the local market. The cat put the boots on, picked up the bag, and left right away.

When the cat reached a forest, he put some fresh grass in the bottom of the bag and set it on the ground. Then he hid and waited until a rabbit entered the trap. The cat quickly tied up the bag with the rabbit inside, threw the sack over his shoulder, and set off for the palace.

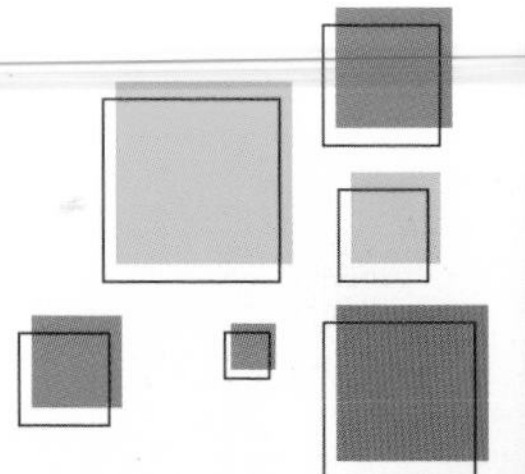

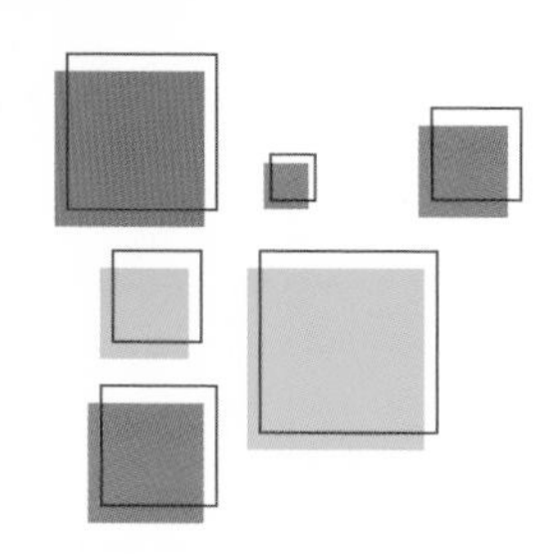

When he reached the palace, the cat asked to see the king. He planned to speak to the ruler on behalf of his master, whom he called the Marquis of Carabas.

Standing before the king, the cat pulled the rabbit out of his sack and said, “Your majesty, the Marquis of Carabas sends you this gift.”

“Give him my thanks,” said the king.

The cat bowed before the king and left.

Then the cat went to a cornfield and put a handful of grains into the bottom of the bag. He caught two birds, and then returned to the palace.

The cat said to the king, “The Marquis of Carabas sends you these birds as another gift.”

“This is a very fine gift,” said the king. “Thank the Marquis on my behalf.”

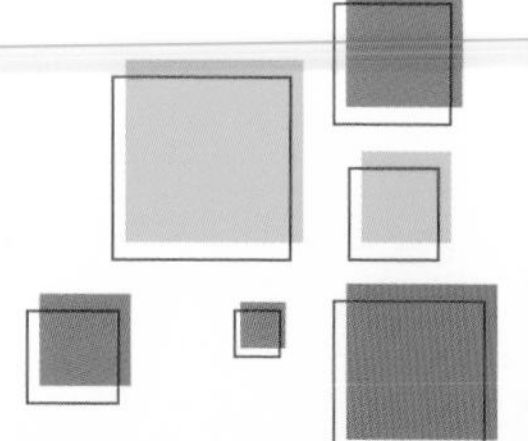

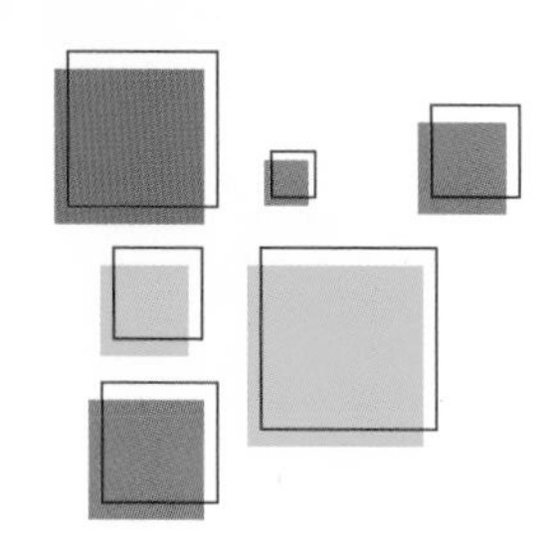

For three months, the cat gave the king many more gifts, saying they were from the Marquis of Carabas. The king thanked him sincerely each time.

One day, the cat heard the king and his daughter, a beautiful princess, making plans to go for a walk along the river.

The cat returned to his master and told him, “Master, you must do as I say! Go down to the river, remove your clothes, and take a bath.”

The young man had grown to trust the cat, and he did as he was told.

When the king and his daughter approached, the cat began to cry out, “Help! The Marquis of Carabas is drowning!”

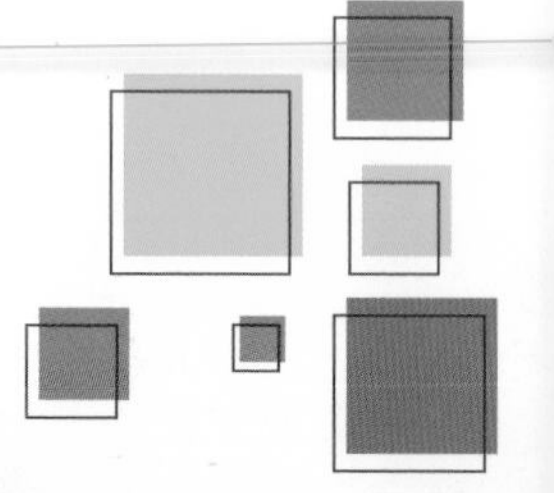

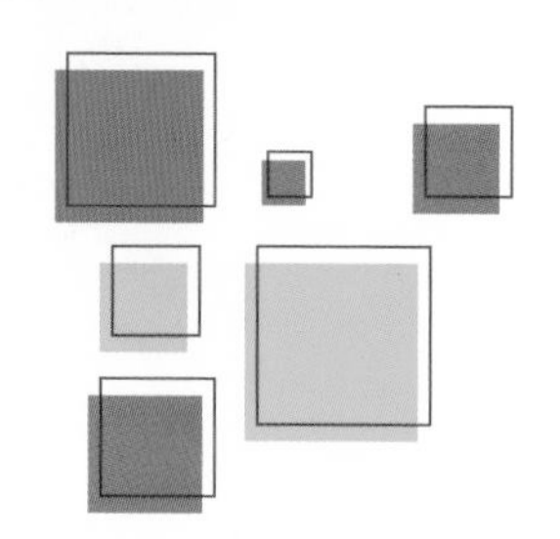

The king heard the cat shouting. He sent three guards to pull the young man out of the river.

"Help!" shouted the cat, who had hidden the young man's clothes under a stone. "Thieves have stolen the Marquis's clothes!"

The king made the most elegantly dressed nobleman in his group give his clothes to the young man.

"I am pleased to finally meet you, Marquis of Carabas!" said the king.

"I'm the lucky one, your majesty!" said the young man, who kept glancing at the princess. The young woman could not stop looking at the young man, either.

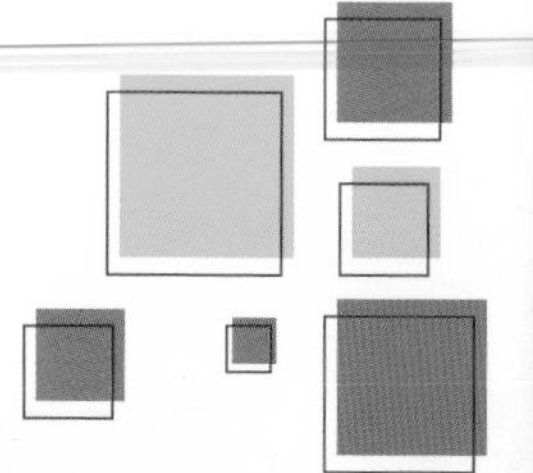

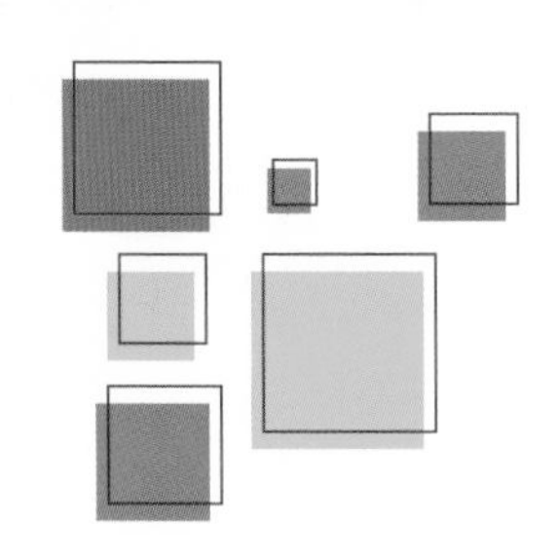

The king turned to the young man. “We’re tired of walking,” he said. “Get into our carriage, and we’ll ride.”

“Please, your highness,” pleaded the cat. “Would you be so kind as to visit the Marquis of Carabas’s castle? It is down this road a few more miles.”

“We would be honored to be your guests,” the king said to the young man.

Meanwhile, the cat ran ahead of the carriage. He came across peasants cutting hay. He said to them, “If you don’t tell the king that these meadows belong to the Marquis of Carabas, I will claw at your eyes!”

The carriage went by, and the king asked, “Good men, who owns this beautiful land?”

“It belongs to the Marquis of Carabas,” the peasants replied nervously.

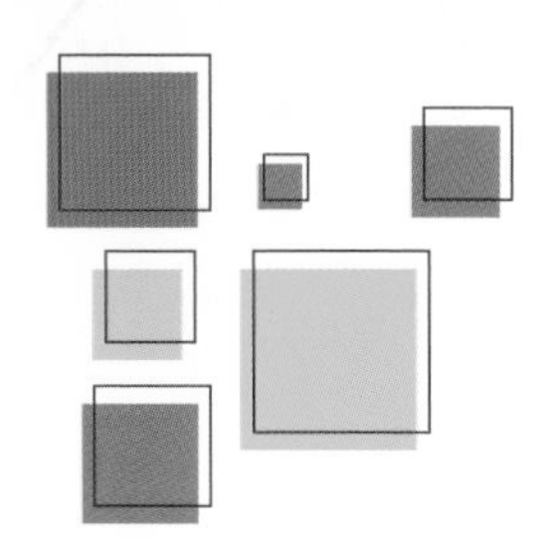

The cat ran ahead and met some farmers. He said to them, “If you don’t tell the king that this corn belongs to the Marquis of Carabas, I will scratch at your feet so you cannot work!”

Soon the carriage reached the farmers. “Whose beautiful cornfields are these?” asked the king.

“They belong to the Marquis of Carabas,” the farmers quickly replied.

The cat ran ahead and did this many more times. At the end of the trip, the king was amazed by how much beautiful land the Marquis of Carabas owned.

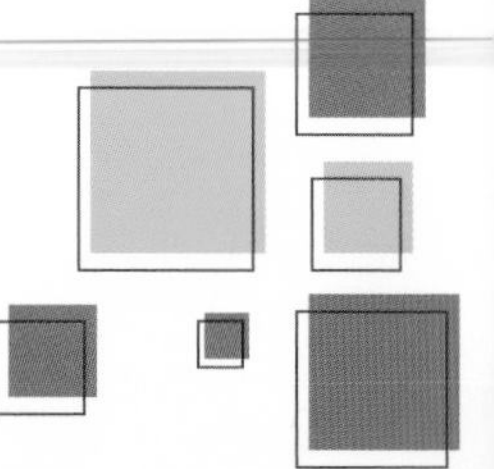

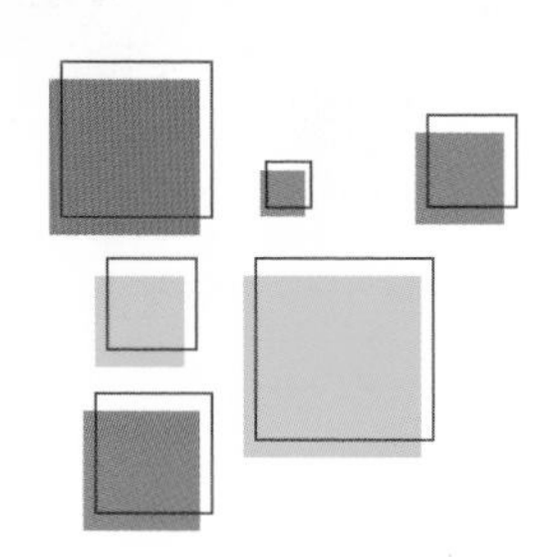

The cat ran and ran until he came to a large castle where a very rich ogre lived.

He asked to meet the ogre, saying he admired the monster. The ogre, who was vain, welcomed him.

"Is it true that you can change yourself into any animal?" the cat asked the ogre.

"I most certainly can!" the ogre replied. "Name any animal, and I will change into it for you."

"Can you change into a lion?" the cat asked.

Zap! The ogre changed into a lion. The cat pretended to be frightened and jumped onto the cabinet.

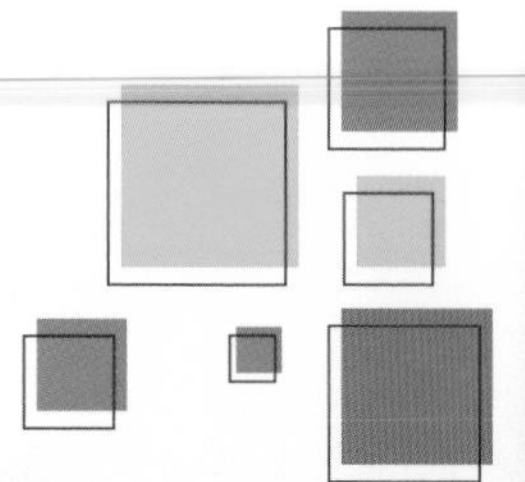

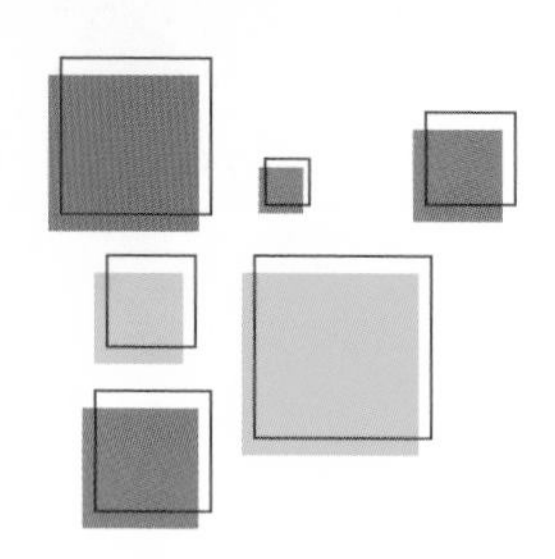

The ogre changed back into himself. "Now do you believe me?" he asked.

"I'm not sure," said the cat, leaping down from the cabinet.

"What do you mean?" asked the ogre.

"Well, it's easy to change into an animal that is your own size," said the cat. "But it's much harder to change into a smaller animal, like a mouse."

"Oh really?" said the ogre.

Zap! He changed himself into a mouse.

The ogre didn't even have the chance to twitch his little mouse tail before the cat pounced on him and ate him.

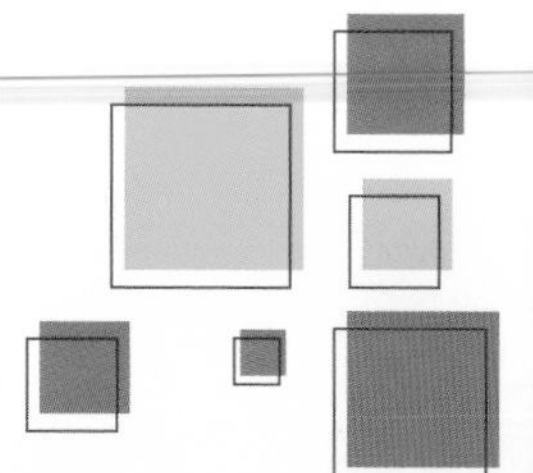

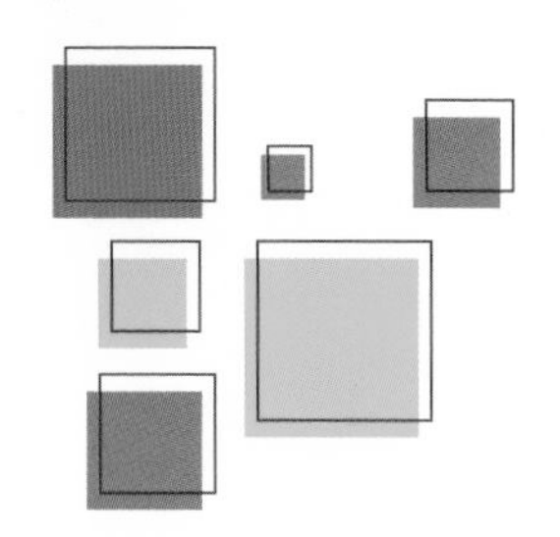

Meanwhile, the king's carriage had arrived at the castle. The cat ran to the gate and bowed.

"Welcome to Marquis of Carabas's castle, your highness!" the cat said.

"Marquis, is this really your castle?" the king asked in amazement.

"If the cat says it is, then yes!" said the young man, smiling. He helped the princess get out of the carriage by offering her his hand.

As they strolled through the palace, they came to a very large hall. A grand table was filled with rich and delicious food.

"What a magnificent feast you have prepared for us!" said the king.

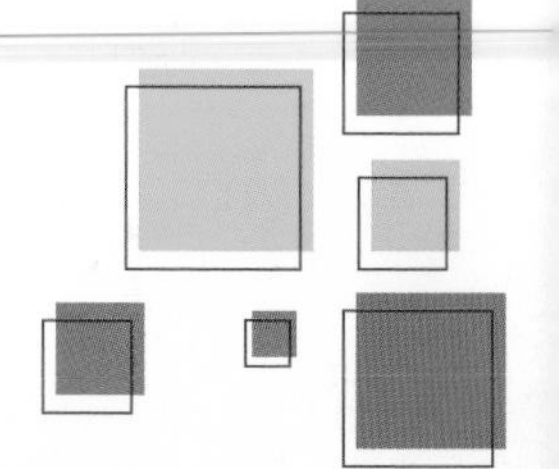

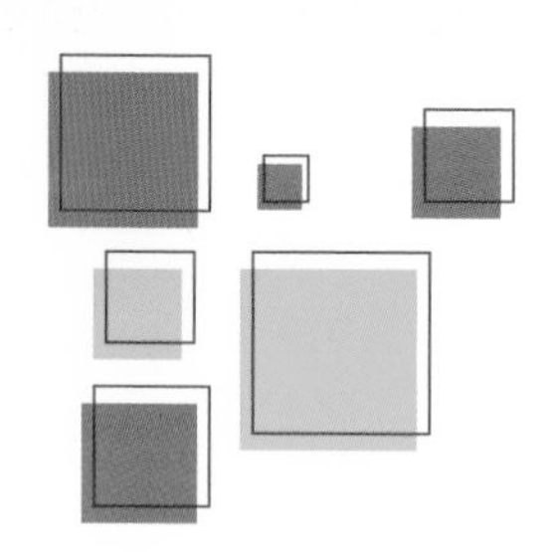

They ate and ate until they were full. At the end of the meal, the king asked, "Would you like to marry my daughter, Marquis of Carabas?"

"Only if she wants to, your majesty," said the young man.

The princess smiled and looked at the young man. "I do! I want to marry you so very much!" she said.

And so the young couple were married and lived happily ever after.

As for the cat, he spent his days hunting mice in the castle — just for fun.

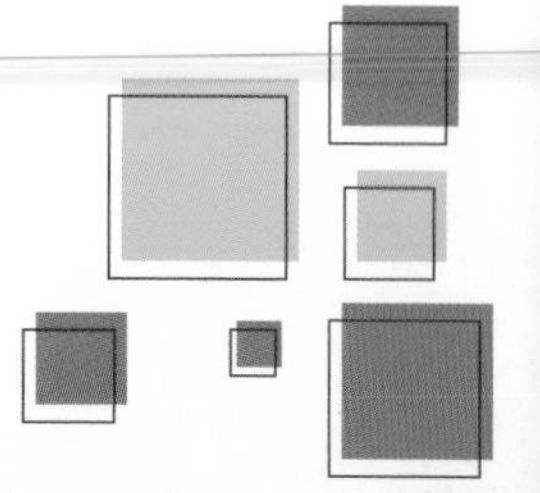

1. Were you surprised that the cat used the bag for a trap? What else could he have used to trap animals?

2. Why did the cat give the king gifts on behalf of his master?

3. Do you think the cat was good or bad? Explain your answer.

4. Puss was a pet to his master. Do you have a pet? What special things does your pet do for you?

delicious (di-LISH-uhss)—very pleasing to taste

disappointed (diss-uh-POIN-tid)—felt let down because something did not go as expected

elegantly (EL-uh-guhnt-lee)—in a graceful and lovely way

majesty (MAJ-uh-stee)—a name for a king or queen

ogre (OH-gur)—a cruel giant or monster

peasants (PEZ-uhnts)—people who work on farms

sincerely (sin-SEER-lee)—in a way that is honest and truthful

Fairy tales have been told for hundreds of years. Most fairy tales share certain elements, or pieces. Once you learn about these elements, you can try writing your own fairy tales.

Element 1: The Characters

Characters are the people, animals, or other creatures in the story. They can be good or evil, silly or serious. Can you name the characters in *Puss in Boots*? The main characters are the cat, his owner, the king, the princess, and the ogre.

Element 2: The Setting

The setting tells us *when* and *where* a story takes place. The *when* of the story could be a hundred years ago or a hundred years in the future. There may be more than one *where* in a story. You could go from a house to a school to a park. In *Puss in Boots*, the story says it happened "once upon a time." Usually this means that it takes place many years ago. And *where* does it take place? Most of the story takes place in the countryside and the ogre's castle.

Element 3: The Plot

Think about what happens in the story. You are thinking about the plot, or the action of the story. In fairy tales, the action begins nearly right away. In *Puss in Boots*, the plot begins on the first page when the dying father asks to speak to his sons. The father says, "I'm leaving the mill to my eldest son. To my second son, I'm leaving my donkey. And to my third son. I'm leaving the cat." And the story takes off from there!

Element 4: Magic

Did you know that all fairy tales have an element of magic? The magic is what makes a fairy tale different from other stories. Often, the magic comes in the form of a character that doesn't exist in real life, such as a giant, a scary witch, or in the case of *Puss in Boots*, a talking cat and an ogre.

Element 5: A Happy Ending

Years ago, fairy tales ended on a sad note, but today, most fairy tales have a happy ending. Readers like knowing that the hero of the story has beaten the villain. Did *Puss in Boots* have a happy ending? Of course! The young man married the princess and they "lived happily ever after." And we can't forget about the cat, who spent his days hunting mice in the castle.

Now that you know the basic elements of a fairy tale, try writing your own! Create characters, both good and bad. Decide when and where their story will take place to give them a setting. Now put them into action during the plot of the story. Don't forget that you need some magic! And finally, give the hero of your story a happy ending.

Roberto Piumini lives and works in Italy. He has worked with children as both a teacher and a theater actor/entertainer. He credits these experiences for inspiring the youthful language of his many books. With his crisp and imaginative way of dealing with every kind of subject, he keeps charming his young readers. His award-winning books, for both children and adults, have been translated into many languages.

When Francesca Chessa was four years old, she saw a film about the artist Michelangelo. Afterward she began drawing inside her wardrobe closet, imagining she was painting the Sistine Chapel. Eventually Chessa studied architecture, but she realized she would rather paint animals and the things that surrounded her. She began illustrating books in 1997. Her studio is colorful, full of books, and overlooks a small courtyard garden.

More Tales to Treasure

Open a Storybook Classic and experience the world of traditional fairy tales told through simple prose and splendid artwork. These safe and inventive picture books feature beautiful and whimsical illustrations that will charm young and old alike.